APR - - 2016

ELOISE

IN

MOSCOW

KAY THOMPSON'S

ELOISE

IN

MOSCOW

DRAWINGS BY
HILARY KNIGHT

LITTLE SIMON
New York   London   Toronto   Sydney   New Delhi

LITTLE SIMON

AN IMPRINT OF SIMON & SCHUSTER CHILDREN'S PUBLISHING DIVISION
1230 AVENUE OF THE AMERICAS, NEW YORK, NEW YORK 10020
FIRST LITTLE SIMON BOOK AND CD EDITION OCTOBER 2015
FOR INFORMATION ABOUT SPECIAL DISCOUNTS FOR BULK PURCHASES, PLEASE
CONTACT SIMON & SCHUSTER SPECIAL SALES AT
1-866-506-1949 OR BUSINESS@SIMONANDSCHUSTER.COM.
THE SIMON & SCHUSTER SPEAKERS BUREAU
CAN BRING AUTHORS TO YOUR LIVE EVENT.
FOR MORE INFORMATION OR TO BOOK AN EVENT CONTACT
THE SIMON & SCHUSTER SPEAKERS BUREAU
AT 1-866-248-3049 OR VISIT OUR WEBSITE
AT WWW.SIMONSPEAKERS.COM.
MANUFACTURED IN CHINA 0815 SCP
2 4 6 8 10 9 7 5 3 1
ISBN 978-1-4814-5155-0
ISBN 978-1-4424-4325-9 (EBOOK)

They were expecting me

and this freezing wind was blowing and this snow was flying in this blizzard

and these people with all of these boots on
took us and stamped us and whisked us around
They didn't examine our luggage
They knew what was in it

Here's the secret password
No Comprendo

Moscow is Russian

The Rolls was waiting

It is the only sports car
I will drive in a
Russian Blizzard
My grandmother had it sent in
by rail
She wanted us to be
comfortable

You only go to Moscow once

And there we were in the middle of Moscow all by ourselves alone
winding around in this snow
Actually we hadn't planned to stay too long

So I said to this driver
"To the Americanski Embassyski pajalasta"
which is
"To the American Embassy please"
and he said "Da"
which is yes
and I said
"Da"
He was Russian
I speak the language fluently
I turned on my radio and got this music from Helsinki

Everybody watches everybody in Moscow

I left my card

Skipperdee developed
this nervous cough
so we had to send
him to New York to the Plaza
by diplomatic
pouch
He was glad to go

My mother knows the ambassador

Here's who I am
Little Miss Diplomat

I always stay at the National whenever I am in Moscow
which is on the corner of Gorky Street if you know where that is

Actually
they were not absolutely glad to see us
and some of us whispered "Ooooooo Nanny"
and we walked into the hotelski

It was rawther chilly

The lobby is different and smells like chicken

Some people were speaking Russian
I let them think I didn't understand

Here's what they don't have
candy counter or
movie magazines
for lords sake
The elevator is absolutely small

You have to be careful of what you do and say in Moscow
otherwise they will swoop down on you and snip-snap at
your wrists and send your radio to Copenhagen by rail

so I said
to these ladies
"Hello I am me ELOISE"
and they said
"Nyet Nyet Nyet Nyet Nyet" which is no
We do not speak the same language
They give you your key
Here's who else they give it to
everybody

All of our letters had come unglued
They have quite a few portraits

We were in 235
at the top of the stairs

Actually
you can have any key you want

and
oh my lord these ladies followed us in with our luggage
and stood there and looked us over

and did this giggling to each other and when they went out we said
"Ooooooo Nanny here we are in Moscow"
and Nanny said
"Da Da Da"
and Weenie said
"Da"
Here's what I said
"Definitely Da"
And while we were
barely unpacking
and looking for these
spies
all of these
other people
began to come
into our room
that we didn't
even know
who they were
and we said
"Nyet Nyet Nyet
what are you doing?"
and they were not
even listening
to us and they
were just
walking around
and picking up
the telephone
and talking and
putting it down
and walking out
with these hats on

But they didn't take
our camera

Here's what you have to watch out for
A Russian is not bashful

So if you are this diplomat
here's what you absolutely cannot do in Moscow

stand around in your long underwear
and talk about your mole

There are quite a few strangers

If you have this secret
tell it to the revolving door

They have purple ink

Here's what there is absolutely
none of in Moscow
Privacy

None of our luggage was missing

Our room looked out onto the Kremlin of course
which is this palace across the street
and these Russian pigeons were clacking themselves against our window
and doing all of this groaning in this foreign language
Then some of us said

"Oooooooooooo Nanny let's call
Russian room service"
which is BUФET
and Nanny said
"Da Da Da jolly good idea"
So I pressed this pink button
and when this waiter came
with these glasses on him
he said
"Pajalasta"
and I said
"Pajalasta
we would like one turkish coffee
pajalasta"
and he said
"Pajalasta"
and I said
"Not black kawfyeh
Black kawfyeh nyet"
and sort of bent my head
and did this slight adagio
with my left hand
And he said
"Nyet nyet pajalasta nyet"
and I said
"But Tooourkeeeeeeeeesh kawfyeh Da?
Tooooooooooourkeeeeeeeeeeesh kawfyeh
Do you understand? Da?"
and he looked through his glasses
and shook his head and coughed
and said
"Pajalasta" and walked out
and I bowed and said
"Pajalasta and spasibo"
which is thank you

I am happy to speak Russian whenever
they do not speak English

BUФET has the best food in Moscow

We did not have to call the doctor

I always take a bawth
in my raccoon hat in case the water is cold
but the flaps have to be absolutely down

The tub is as big as the Moscow River
So it is wise to hold your head up

I sang "Ochi Chornya" rawther sweetly for Nanny
but I had to stop because it hurt Weenie's ears

The water is Russian so I brushed my teeth
with
pear lemonade and apple lemonade
Actually I preferred
the pear

Here's what they don't have
Quite a few things

You can get your cleaning done in Helsinki

Everybody knows what everybody's doing
every minute of the day in Moscow

Here's what you are
never alone

We put on our woollies to protect us from the freezing weather

Then Nanny said
"Let's go have
some of that delicious Russian
food food food"
and we all said
"Oh definitely Da"
We were absolutely starving

This man was in his pajamas
in the hall with
his hat on
It was rawther unusual

You can't even dine
with your boots on
in Moscow

Weenie's coat
was made of porcupine
which was rawther sweet
He got it especially for the trip
They treated him like a dog

And here's the thing of it
When you go out of your room you can
lock your door and leave
your key with these ladies if you want to but
actually you do not need to bother
because the minute you go out
somebody else
goes right in
for lords sake

There is no manager

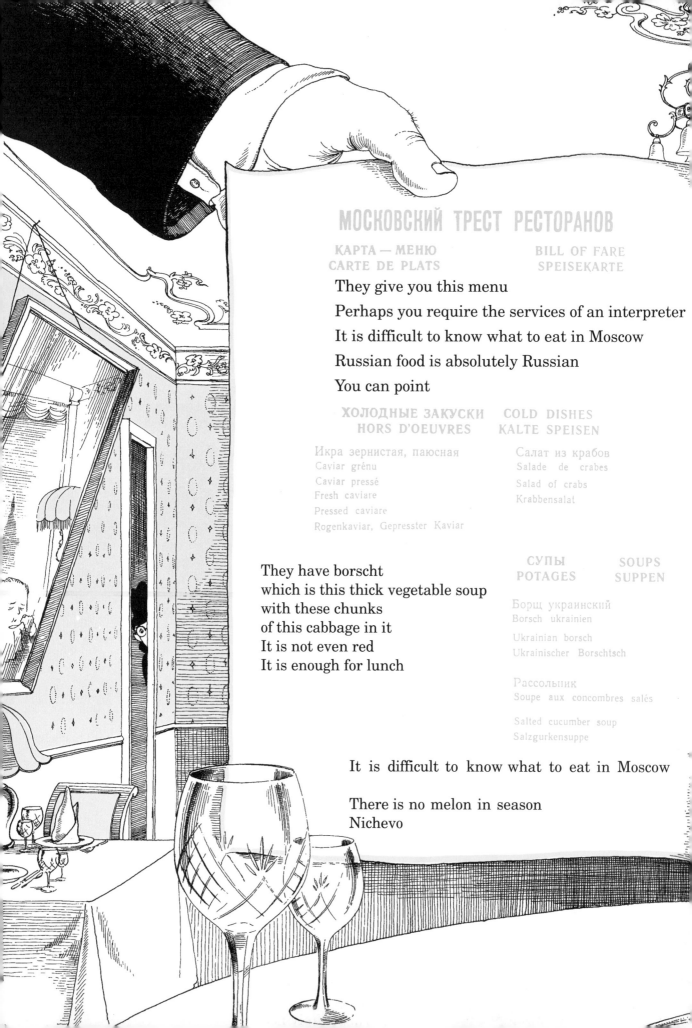

МОСКОВСКИЙ ТРЕСТ РЕСТОРАНОВ

КАРТА — МЕНЮ   BILL OF FARE
CARTE DE PLATS   SPEISEKARTE

They give you this menu

Perhaps you require the services of an interpreter

It is difficult to know what to eat in Moscow

Russian food is absolutely Russian

You can point

ХОЛОДНЫЕ ЗАКУСКИ   COLD DISHES
HORS D'OEUVRES   KALTE SPEISEN

Икра зернистая, паюсная   Салат из крабов
Caviar grénu   Salade de crabes
Caviar pressé   Salad of crabs
Fresh caviare   Krabbensalat
Pressed caviare
Rogenkaviar, Gepresster Kaviar

СУПЫ   SOUPS
POTAGES   SUPPEN

They have borscht
which is this thick vegetable soup   Борщ украинский
with these chunks   Borsch ukrainien
of this cabbage in it
It is not even red   Ukrainian borsch
It is enough for lunch   Ukrainischer Borschtsch

Рассольник
Soupe aux concombres salés

Salted cucumber soup
Salzgurkensuppe

It is difficult to know what to eat in Moscow

There is no melon in season
Nichevo

РЯЧИЕ МЯСНЫЕ БЛЮДА
ENTREES
ARME FLEISCHSPEISEN

ицель отбивной из свинины
alope de porc panée
ener pork shnitzel
ener Schweinsschnitzel

шлык по-кавказски
chlyk à la caucasienne

casian shashlyk
aschlyk auf Kaukasische Art

I changed my mind rawther a lot

I usually decided on the curd cakes
although sometimes
I decided on the shashlik
but most of the time I decided on
this black caviar from the Caspian Sea
which is fish eggs

БЛЮДА МОЛОЧНЫЕ
И МУЧНЫЕ
PLATS FARINEUX ET DE
LAIT
FARINACEOUS AND MILK
FOODS
MILCH-UND MEHLSPEISEN

Сырники со сметаной
Beignets de fromage blanc à la crème

Curd-cakes with sour-cream
Milchkäsebuletten mit Sauersahne

Nanny ordered an egg
and it had a feather on it
So she changed her mind and had
Beef Stroganoff Sturgeon and a
Blintz
Weenie had schnitzel

ПИТКИ WARM DRINKS
ISSONS HEISSE GETRÄNKE

й с лимоном   Tea with lemon
è au citron   Tee mit Zitrone

фе черный   Black coffee
fé noir   Schwarzer Kaffee

Here's what we wished we had
Planked Medallion of Beef Tenderloin
with sauce Béarnaise
and Fresh Vegetables Maison
and strawberries in cream

СЛАДКИЕ БЛЮДА
DESSERTS
SÜSSE SPEISEN

Пломбир сливочный
Glace à la Plombière

Plombière icecream
Rahmgefrorenes à la Plombière

Russian tea is
weak weak weak

Here's what you cannot do in Moscow
Charge it pajalasta and thank you very much
Nobody has any business in Moscow

If you are a diplomat you can say the food is good
Actually
it is absolutely not

We had to hurry to meet our guide
because you absolutely have to have one
or you will get lost
which is fine because they speak English

and she will tell you what **IS POSSIBLE**
and what **IS NOT POSSIBLE** in Moscow

so we said
"Well hello my dear" and smiled or so
and cheerfully extended our hand

and she said
"WHAT WOULD YOU LIKE TO SEE?"

and we said
"Well oh my lord
we have come for the weekend
and we would like to see
the circus
a czar
a kazatzki
and a
Charlotte Russe"

**"IT IS NOT POSSIBLE WITHOUT TICKETS
AT SERVICE BUREAU DAY IN ADVANCE
IS POSSIBLE WILL NOT BE POSSIBLE"**

and we said
"Oh da"
and she said
**"YOU WILL COME AND PAY ATTENTION
I WILL GET CAR"**

Her name was Zhenka
We called her Zhenk for short
She was our interpreter
She was Russian
She has an accent

Weenie said
"Ooooooo Nanny someone is following us"
and Nanny said
"Nyet Nyet Nyet is not possible"
But we didn't turn around

I never go to Moscow without my telescope

When we came out of this hotel
she had rawther a lot to say
"IS POSSIBLE TO SEE HERE
SPACIOUS SQUARE
LAID OUT IN CONNECTION WITH CITY RECONSTRUCTION PROJECT
IN FORMER DAYS IS RIDING SCHOOL"

There was this bitterly wind and this frost and this stinging was in our face
and these people were staring

There are absolutely nothing but feet
Some of them have holes
Moscow snow sticks and squeaks

If you are a diplomat here is what is not possible
snowballs
Then Zhenk said
"NOW WE GO ON TOUR OF CITY"

and we said "Definitely Da" and turned up this music from Helsinki

Zhenk raised her voice
**"IS POSSIBLE TO SEE HERE GORKY STREET
WHICH IS CAPITAL'S MAIN THREE-KILOMETER ARTERY"**

"IS POSSIBLE TO SEE HERE GASTRONOMES"

**"IS POSSIBLE TO SEE HERE
CENTRAL TELEGRAPH OFFICE"**

"IS POSSIBLE TO SEE HERE
SOVIETSKAYA SQUARE
PLEASURE GARDEN WITH STATUES
IN FORMER DAYS WAS EMPTY LOT"

"IS POSSIBLE TO SEE HERE LEONTYEVSKY LANE #5
WHICH IS HOUSE OF STANISLAVSKY
WHERE CHEKHOV LIVED"

"THAT HOUSE IS CHEKHOV
THAT HOUSE IS STANISLAVSKY IF YOU WANT TO SEE IT
NO YOU CANNOT IS RECONSTRUCTION"

"THAT HOUSE IS PUSHKIN WHEN
HE MARRIED HER HE LIVED IN
THAT HOUSE

IS PUSHKIN MONUMENT

ON OPPOSITE SIDE IS TOLSTOY HOUSE"

"IS NOT POSSIBLE
TO SEE HERE
WATER WORKS
GAS HOUSE
POWER HOUSE
IS RECONSTRUCTION"

"IS NOT POSSIBLE TO
SEE HERE
RECONSTRUCTION
IS BLIZZARD"

"IS POSSIBLE TO SEE HERE COMMISSION STORE"

"IS POSSIBLE TO SEE HERE BEAUTY SALON"

"IS POSSIBLE TO SEE HERE LAMP SHADES"

"IS POSSIBLE TO SEE HERE HATS"

Zhenk does absolutely nothing but talk

Zhenk pointed to the right
"THAT IS REGION OF RECONSTRUCTION"

"NICHOLAS I WAS BUILT IN 1801"

"ON LEFT IS ACADEMY OF SCIENCE"

**"ON RIGHT SIDE IS BUILDING
REFERRING TO EIGHTEENTH CENTURY"**

**"IS NOT POSSIBLE TO SEE ZOO
IS BLIZZARD"**

**"IS POSSIBLE TO SEE HERE
MOSCOW UNIVERSITY"**

**"IS POSSIBLE TO SEE HERE
BOLSHEVIKY CONFECTIONERY"**

**"IS POSSIBLE TO SEE HERE
LENIN STADIUM"**

**"IS NOT POSSIBLE TO SEE HERE
ON OPPOSITE SIDE OF HIGHWAY
GATEWAY OF TREE-SHADED
ALLEY LEADING TO GRANDSTANDS
OF MOSCOW RACE COURSE"**

We passed these little log houses
and came to these birch trees
which were absolutely tall

And Zhenk cleared her throat
and said
"IN FORMER DAYS WAS PALACE OF PRINCE YUSSOUPOV
ALEXANDER I WAS CZAR WHO REIGNED RUSSIA
WHEN IT HAD WAR WITH NAPOLEON"

I took this picture of Weenie among the birches
I was not arrested
Not all Russian dogs are diplomats

It was colder inside than out
which was 10 below zero
centigrade of course

The trip was rawther tiring

You can hum with your eyes closed and
no one will hear you
Sometimes I take a nap and forget where I am

On the way back to the city
some of us were yawning
and Zhenk said
"YOU ARE TIRED"
And we said
"Is possible Zhenk"
just to make her feel good
and she said
"WE ARE NEVER TIRED
WE ARE STRONGER THAN NATURE"
and we said "Is not possible" and
we all laughed

Some days she spoke to us

some days not

We skibbled home to change our gloves
and met Zhenk in the lobby
at 7:30

And Zhenk said
"NOW WE GO TO KHUDOZHESTVENNY TEATR LANE
IS MOSCOW ART THEATRE
TREASURE TROVE RUSSIAN NATIONAL DRAMA"

We saw *Anna Karenina*
It was sad

We had an orange
for 10 rubles
in the interval

"NOW WE GO TO
CENTRAL PUPPET THEATRE"
We laughed rawther loud
They were comical
I was 5 rubles
Nanny was 18

We had a little black caviar
from the Caspian Sea
in the interval

"NOW WE GO TO
TCHAIKOVSKY HALL"
They asked me to play
I played Chopsticks in F♯
They went absolutely wild
I waved Dasvidanya
which is see you later

I am accustomed to a Baldwin

Zhenk said
"NOW WHAT DO YOU WANT TO SEE?"
and we said
"Oh Zhenk we want to
see the circus"
and Zhenk said
"WHEN ARE YOU LEAVING MOSCOW?"
and we said
"We are leaving Sunday"
and she said
"CIRCUS OPENS MONDAY"

And Nanny said
"Oh stop this mucking about
we're going to the
circus tonight"
And we did

Here's what we saw
a hippopotamus and
a snake

Here's what you cawnt
let them do
run you up the wall
Zhenk didn't like
the circus

We had salami sandwiches
and a little of this
black caviar from the
Caspian Sea in the interval
There are absolutely
nothing but
intervals

We left early
and went home and
went to sleep and
dreamed of steaming
hot cornbread
from "21"

It was delicious

Next day Zhenk arrived
bright and early
singing "Rudolph the Red-Nosed Reindeer"
We said
"Hi Zhenk"
Zhenk stopped singing
and said
**"IS BLIZZARD
WE GO TO
SUBWAY"**

She told us all about it
**"THE MOSCOW METRO IS SPACIOUS
AND ITS MAGNIFICENT DECORATIONS
ADD TO SENSATION OF AIRY SPACE
PASSENGER IS SPARED OPPRESSIVE
"SUBWAY" FEELING EVERY STATION
IS OF DISTINCTIVE DETAIL
FOR INSTANCE
1. PLOSHSCHAD SVERDLOVA STATION
IS THEATRICAL MOTIFS AND COLUMNS
AND CHANDELIERS
2. PLOSHSCHAD REVOLUTSII STATION
IS STATUES
3. KIESKAYA STATION IS COLORED
MARBLE WALLS
4. MAYKOVSKAYA STATION IS
STAINLESS STEEL
5. NOVOKUZNETSKAYA STATION IS
STUCCO BAS RELIEFS OF BATTLE
SCENES AND MEDALLIONS
6. PAVELETSKAYA STATION IS A
MOSAIC MILITARY PARADE
7. IZMAILOVSKAYA STATION IS
GLORY TO PARTISANS
8. KOMSOMOLSKAYA-KOLTSEVAYA
STATION IS 72 OCTAHEDRAL PYLONS
AND MOSAICS MARBLE GRANITE
JASPER
9. KIEVSKAYA-KOLTSEVAYA STATION
IS PRECIOUS STONES AND SMALT
FRAGMENTS
10. NOVOSLOBODSKAYA STATION IS
32 VIGNETTES OF STAINED GLASS"**

If you do not understand simply nod your head
and say "No Comprendo"
Here's how many times I've nodded our head so far
16

The Russian subway is absolutely
clean and looks like a bank
There is absolutely nothing but
marble

Here's the thing of it
there is not one singley ad
so everyone sleeps
I played my bongos
It was rawther effective
Actually
I preferred the stained
glass

We had to come up for air

Then Zhenk said
**"IS POSSIBLE TO SEE HERE GUM
THE EMPORIUM BETWEEN
KUIBISHCHEV AND OCTOBER 25TH
STREET BUILT IN 1893
AFTER RECONSTRUCTION"**

Which is this department
store that has this dome
and this ice cream and
oh my lord
it is absolutely
savage with these people
who are knocking you with
their elbows and running
and turning around and
bumping you and tossing
you along to where
you do not want
to go and swarming around

We didn't do much shopping
We couldn't find what we
were looking for which was
this Siberian tiger
they were sold out
Actually there is quite
a crowd

"IN FORMER DAYS
IS POSSIBLE TO
SEE HERE
MARKET PLACE
RED SQUARE
IMMEDIATE NEIGHBORHOOD
OF KREMLIN
SCENE OF MOMENTOUS EVENTS IN
RUSSIAN HISTORY AND IS
POINT OF
CONVERGENCE OF HIGHWAYS
LEADING THROUGH MOSCOW'S
CEASELESS NOISY
AND BRISK COMMERCE"

"IN THE SIXTEENTH CENTURY WAS MOAT RUNNING ALONG KREMLIN WALL"

BOROVITZKAYA TOWER

WATER SUPPLY TOWER

ALEXANDER PARK

"KREMLIN WALLS ENCO

CHAMBER of ARMS

I
was
an
angel
all
over
the
Kremlin

**"THE STRIKING CONTOURS OF ANCIENT KREMLIN MEDIEVAL CITADEL
HAVE COME TO BE A VERITABLE SYMBOL OF SOVIET MOSCOW"**

TROITZKAYA TOWER

HOTEL NATIONAL

AREA 26 HECTARES

THE ARSENAL

THE KREMLIN PALACE

TEREM PALACE

GRANOVITAYA CHAMBER

CATHEDRAL ANNUNCIATION

We said "Ooooo Nanny
look at us
inside the Kremlin wall"

"IN FORMER DAYS IS POSSIBLE TO SEE HERE TREES"

MOSCOW RIVER

When we came out
the snow hit us in the
face and we had to hold
our head against this
wind that was flurring
and blusting at us
Zhenk said **"NOW IS COLD
WEATHER IN MOSCOW"**

There were these little snow
ladies shoveling the
snow as fast as
it was falling and
they wouldn't let
us take their
picture because
they had on their
summer dresses

and oh my lord we turned
around and right across
the street was
Red Square
And Zhenk said **"I WILL TELL YOU EVERYTHING"** and she did

"NOW WE WILL GO INSIDE
AND I WILL TELL YOU ABOUT KREMLIN
AND YOU WILL LISTEN
DO YOU UNDERSTAND?"
and we said "Oh da"

They stand in line for everything in Moscow
There are absolutely nothing but tombs

SPASSKAYA TOWER

ST. BASIL'S CATHEDRAL

Here's what they
have in the Kremlin
armor
Easter eggs
icons
and clocks

Nanny said
"The landscaping needs
attending to and plawnts"

Then Zhenk said
**"IS POSSIBLE TO SEE ON SOUTH SIDE
ST. BASIL'S CATHEDRAL
MASTERPIECE RUSSIAN
ARCHITECTURE"**

All these czars
were walking around
and were buried in this marble
Ivan is terrible
and is watching in this tower

"IS POSSIBLE TO SEE HERE GOLD CUPOLAS OF KREMLIN"

You should see Moscow in the night

Nanny and I
took a long walk
across the street
And there were
these little
snow ladies
shoveling this
snow and they
had on these
boots
and their
dresses
were blowing
The brisk air
made our
eyelashes
limp

and
oh my lord
someone was
following us

I was
glad that
I had
brought
my
white
gloves

When we got to our room
this blizzard was hitting against
our window and these pigeons
were absolutely flapping
and hollering
and there we were having our
usual glass of weak tea
and I was having a little of
this black
caviar from the Caspian Sea
on toast
and Nanny was soothing us
with a slight serenadesky
on the balalaika

when all of a sudden
Weenie let out this
shriek of barking
and stood up on his
back legs like Czar
Nicholas I
and started to sniff
and go absolutely wild
and Nanny said
"Pajalasta and Nyet Nyet Nyet"
but Weenie didn't
and he jumped straight up into
the air and onto this bed
and stood there like this
hunter and his ears were absolutely
stiff
and we said
"What is it Weenie dear?
Is it possible that you
are feeling ill or so?"
and he said
"Nyet absolutely Nyet
is not possible
I simply hear this squeaking noise"

And we said
"Oh my lord Weenie dear
what is it?"
and he said
"No Comprendo
let's have a look around"

and oh my lord
we ran around this
room and jumped up
on this bed
and Nanny said
"shhhhhh"
and we said
"shh"
and we were breathing
on each other
and we listened
and we heard these
voices coming out of
this grille
which used to be this
radiator
and some of us ran
and hid behind these
doors in this
cupboard and screamed
and pulled this
rug back and
oh my lord
this piece of wood
in the floor
was absolutely loose
There was a dead moth

Weenie was rawther upset
so I gave him this
bruised apple that
had these warts on it
from the Crimea

Our telephone had quite a bit of static
so we talked about General de Gaulle
to throw them off track

Everybody listens to everything in Moscow

I usually went on my tour of the rooms
in the middle of the night
There was
only one lady on duty

So I gave her a copy of *Life* magazine
with all of these pictures to enjoy
while I picked out the keys to the rooms
that I wanted to investigate through these keyholes or so
She didn't look up

I wore my disguise

No one was aware of the fact that I was a hotel child

Some people were sleeping

but some weren't

Some weren't even yawning

Half of the time I was working in the dark
Every once in a while I thought I heard
someone breathing behind my back

Some of the doors were locked

There were quite a few briefcases in Moscow
but they didn't have anything interesting in them

I left some hyacinth bulbs in
the armoire in 415

I turned off all of the steam
in all of the rooms
It was too hot

Quite a few people were coughing

There was this party in 423
with these commissars
but all they had to eat was
this black caviar from the Caspian Sea

Their voices were rawther loud
and they were hollering

I was under the table
most of the time

I had a little trouble opening 658
I sort of had this feeling that someone
was leaning against the door

If I had too many rooms to visit in one
night
I would usually unlock 543
and simply lie down on this comforter
and read *Pravda* or so

No news is good news

The beds are more than comfortable

If you want to know
what's going on in the next
room simply lie down and listen

Here's what I did a lot of
listening
Here's what I heard
a lot

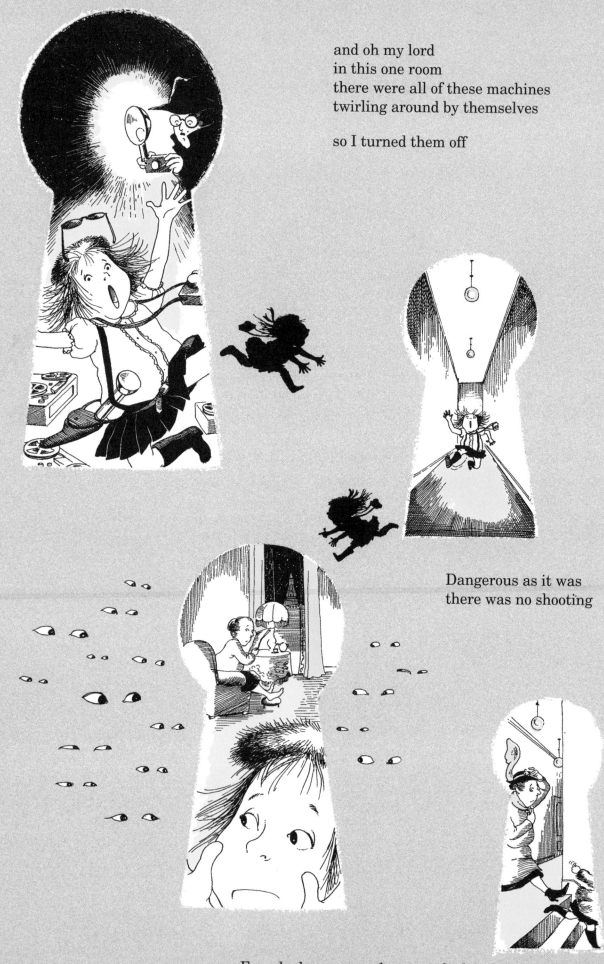

and oh my lord
in this one room
there were all of these machines
twirling around by themselves

so I turned them off

Dangerous as it was
there was no shooting

Everybody can see what everybody's doing in Moscow

We went to
the Aragvi
for dinner
which is
absolutely
Georgian
and oh my lord
we sat in this
balcony
and the
specialty of
the house
is
Tsiplyaka Tabaca
which is this
broiled chicken
on the bricks
which
has been
flattened out
and is
rawther thin

The orchestra is
up on the wall and
everyone is having
this good time
and a red face

I had a little mineral
water or so which is
pronounced
mineral water

They have
paper napkins

Here's what is not allowed
Diner's Club Card

And
oh my lord
you should see
the
pigeons
that hang around
the
Bolshoi
They are wild
about the ballet
and
are absolutely
on point
I did a
pas de deux
with them

It was rawther unusual

Russian pigeons pretend they don't hear you
Their voices are rawther deep

Then
these
pigeons
clinked their ankles
and
pointed their legs
and
jiggled their toes
and
jumped
and
went
absolutely
up
into
the
air
never
to
be
seen
again

This big crowd was pushing itself into us
Not everyone in Moscow is a diplomat

Here's what we did the most
check our coats

Everybody is up in the air in Moscow

I was partially over their heads

In the interval

some people go to
BUϕET
to have ice cream
or
some little
refreshment
to drink
like vodka
or cognac

They had this
black caviar
from the
Caspian Sea
but I was
rawther tired
of it
I would
have had
champagne
but it
was
Russian
Nanny had
several
beers
I had
raisin
cake

They looked at us quite a bit
We were rawther unusual

Then we hurried to the railroad station with our skis and mittens
to take the midnight train for winter sports
There was this absolute crowd
Everyone was hurrying

There were some rawther unusual people

I said Dasvidanya to this snow lady which is see you later
And she said Da Dasvidanya

Our compartment had red plush curtains
and
we had this little Russian czarina supper
and wine and cake and a tangerine and
red fish eggs

We were not hungry anyway

And oh my lord
there was this man that slept with us without a curtain
We left the blue light on
so that we could see what he was doing

I slept with my boots on in case there was going to be this raid
Nanny didn't even take off her corset
The militia were watching

Weenie was my hot-water bottle
The train was an absolute wiggle

When we got there
we took this troika in this bustle of snow with these bells on it
and these horses were smiling and everything was absolute ice
and covered over

I always ride my tricycle whenever I am on the Baltic Sea

I am rawther good at winter sports but I prefer the ski
because this snow and wind goes up your nostrils
and you can hardly breathe or get your breath
It is rawther refreshing
I can do a twistie or a christie whichever you prefer
I am partial to an afternoon blizzard

I slalomed right into
this snowdrift
and I turned up my radio
and we danced the
snow-ladies ballet
to the music from Helsinki

We had hot tea
but no one saw us
There is rawther a lot of ballet in Moscow

Then Nanny said it's time to go
and we said
goodbye to everyone

We went back to our hotel
for the lawst time

and packed our luggage

We said Pajalasta
for the lawst time

and then we drove to the Americanski Embassyski

We said Dasvidanya to Zhenk
and we said when you come
to New York look us up
and gave her a present of
lipstick and oranges
She said it was just what she
wanted and started to hum

She gave us perfume
It was Russian

The ambassador was waiting
for me
I gave him my bongos
He had a message
from my mother for me

And I had this absolutely delicious hamburger
on this darling little roll which was practically
unheard of
to this sweet little child of 6
who had been eating
nothing but curd cakes and borscht

There was a cable from Skipperdee
He got all of our letters
He saves stamps

Then the ambassador said to this spy
who had been following us with this hat on
for lords sake
"Well now what's your report?
What has Eloise been up to in Moscow?
Did she live up to our expectations?"
and I said
"I certainly have
Definitely da"
and the ambassador said to him
"Did she do anything that might create an Incident?
Is the Kremlin wall still standing?
Will there be any international repercussions?"
And I said "Nyet
Definitely Nyet"

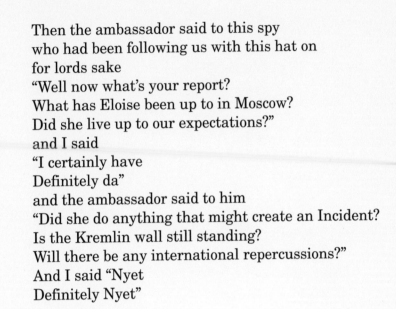

Here's what I have been
this absolutely darling little
sweetnik

And the ambassador smiled
and said
"So long"
and gave us some popcorn
and this spy
sighed and said
"See you later"
which is
Dasvidanya

I can always tell when someone is following me

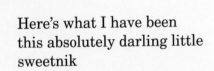

Oh

I could tell you a lot
but I am only six

Kay Thompson (1909-1998) was a singer, dancer, vocal arranger, and coach of many MGM musicals in the 1940's.

The Eloise character grew out of the voice of a precocious six-year-old that Miss Thompson put on to amuse her friends. Collaborating with Hilary Knight on what was an immediate bestseller, Kay Thompson became a literary sensation when *Eloise* was published in 1955. The book has sold more than two million copies to date. Kay Thompson and Hilary Knight created three more Eloise books, *Eloise in Paris*, *Eloise at Christmastime*, and *Eloise in Moscow*, all of which are now to be reissued by Simon & Schuster.

Hilary Knight, son of artist-writers Clayton Knight and Katharine Sturges, was educated the Art Students' League, where he studied with Reginald Ma Besides the Eloise books, Hilary Knight has illustrated over fifty books for children, six of which he wrote himself.

He lives and works in New York City, not far from the Plaza Hot